Paddington's Picnic

written by *Michael Bond*
illustrated by *Nick Ward for Ross Design*

Young Lions
An Imprint of HarperCollinsPublishers

First published in Great Britain 1993 in Young Lions
3 5 7 9 8 6 4 2

Young Lions is an imprint of the Children's Division,
part of HarperCollins Publishers Ltd,
77–85 Fulham Palace Road, Hammersmith,
London W6 8JB

ISBN   0 00 674673-X

Printed and bound in Great Britain by
HarperCollins Manufacturing, Glasgow

Part One

Paddington sat up in bed with a puzzled expression on his face.

Happenings at number thirty-two Windsor Gardens, particularly breakfast, always followed a strict time-table and it was most unusual for anything to wake him so early.

He took a careful look around his room, but everything seemed to be in its place.

Paddington heaved a sigh of relief. He absent-mindedly dipped his paw into the marmalade jar, then pricked up his ears.

There were voices coming from the garden. Several times he heard a door bang,

and then he heard a noise like clinking plates,

followed by the sound of Mr Brown shouting orders.

Ssh, you'll wake Paddington!

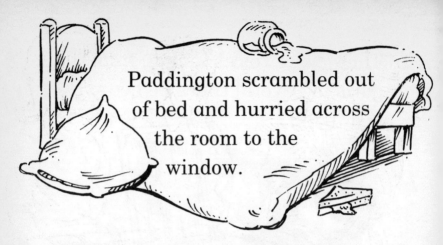

Paddington scrambled out of bed and hurried across the room to the window.

He peered through the glass, then he nearly fell over backwards with astonishment.

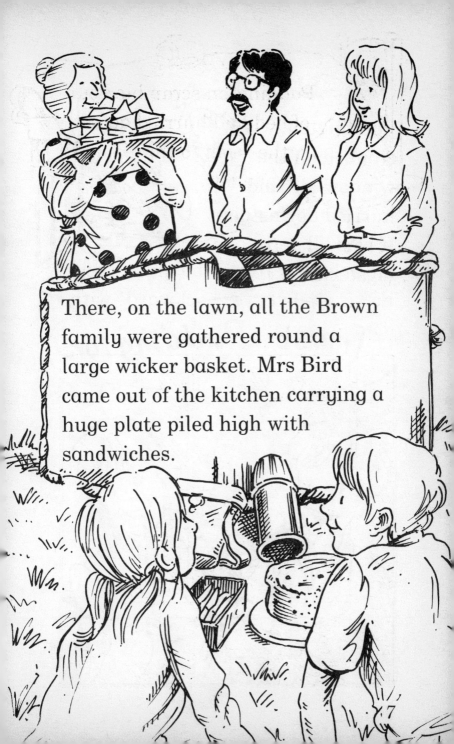

There, on the lawn, all the Brown family were gathered round a large wicker basket. Mrs Bird came out of the kitchen carrying a huge plate piled high with sandwiches.

7

Paddington
climbed off the
window-sill and
hurried downstairs.
It was all very
mysterious.

8

"That bear can smell out a marmalade sandwich a mile away," grumbled Mrs Bird.

"Honestly," said Judy, waving her finger at him. "It was meant to be a surprise. We got up specially early."

Paddington looked from one to the other with growing surprise.

"It's all right, Paddington," laughed Mrs Brown. "We're only going for a picnic on the river."

"And we're having a competition," cried Jonathan, waving a fishing net in the air. "Dad's promised a prize to whoever makes the first catch."

PRIZE *for* THE FIRST *Catch*

Paddington's eyes grew
rounder and rounder.

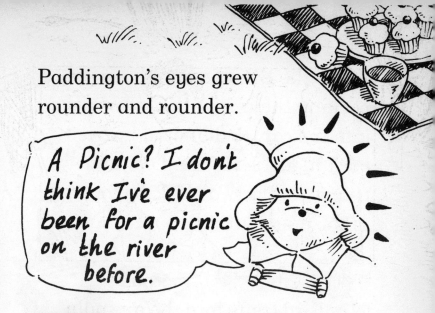

A Picnic? I don't
think I've ever
been for a picnic
on the river
before.

"That's good," said
Mr Brown, twirling his
moustache briskly,
"because you're going
on one now. So hurry
up and eat your
breakfast."

While the Browns were busy packing the rest of the picnic gear into the car, Paddington hurried back indoors. He liked doing new things and he was looking forward to the day's outing.

Mrs Bird came into the dining room.

There were several important
things to be done before he went
out for the day.

First of all there
was his suitcase
to be packed,

then he had to consult his atlas.
Paddington was very keen on
geography and he was interested
in the thought of having a picnic
on the river. It sounded most
unusual.

Mrs Bird adjusted her hat for about the fortieth time.

I don't know why it is, but whenever this family goes any where it always takes enough to keep a regiment for a month.

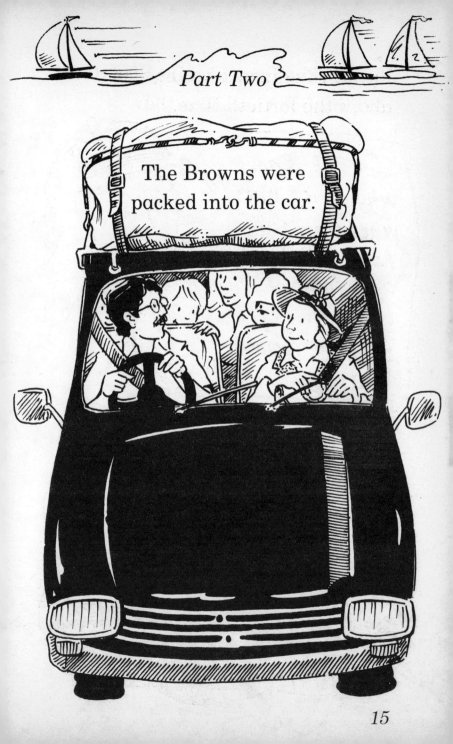

Part Two

The Browns were packed into the car.

Besides the Browns, Mrs Bird and
Paddington, there was the
hamper,

a gramophone,

a pile of records,

a number of parcels

and some fishing nets—not to
mention several sunshades,

a tent

and a pile of cushions.

"Is it much farther?" Mrs Brown asked.

Paddington's leather suitcase was sticking in her back and his old hat, which he insisted on wearing in case of sunstroke, kept tickling the side of her face.

Paddington consulted his map. "I think it's the next turning on the right," he announced, following the route with his paw.

"I do hope so," said Mrs Brown. They had already taken one wrong turning that morning when Paddington had followed a piece of dried marmalade peel on his map by mistake.

Paddington stuck his head out of the window and sniffed.

I think we must be getting near, Mr Brown. I can smell something unusual.

"That's the gas works," said Mr Brown. "The river's on *this* side."

They swept round a corner and
there was a broad expanse of
water.

They all clambered out of the car.
While the others were unloading,
Paddington stood on the water's
edge.

He was most impressed.

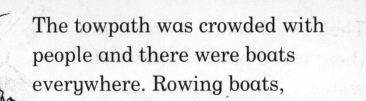

The towpath was crowded with
people and there were boats
everywhere. Rowing boats,

canoes,

punts

and sailing boats,

their white sails
billowing in the wind.

21

As Paddington watched, a steamer
packed with more people swept by.
It sent a large wave shooting
across the water making all the
smaller boats rock.

Everyone on board seemed very
happy. Several of them pointed
towards Paddington and waved.

Paddington raised his hat and
turned to the others. "I think I'm
going to like the river," he
announced.

Part Three

Mrs Brown looked at the row of
boats moored by the landing stage.
It *had* seemed a very good idea to
have a picnic on the river.

But the boats looked awfully
small.

"Are you sure they're safe, Henry?"
she asked, looking at them
nervously.

25

Mr Brown led the way on to the
landing stage.

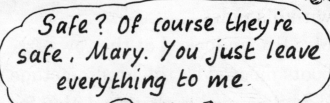

Safe? Of course they're
safe. Mary. You just leave
everything to me.

"I'll put you in charge of all the
ropes and things, Paddington," he
called. "That means you can steer."

"Thank you very much, Mr
Brown," said Paddington,
feeling most important.

He climbed into the boat and carefully examined everything with his paws.

Mr Brown helped the others in.

The boatman's rather busy, so I said we would shove off by ourselves.

Mrs Brown picked Mrs Bird's best sun hat off the floor of the boat.

Mr Brown settled himself on his seat and took a firm grip on the oars.

Here we go. Stand by at the helm, Paddington.

Pull on the ropes. Come on—left paw down.

"Oh, dear," said Mrs Bird nervously. She clutched the side of the boat with one hand and gripped her sunshade with the other. People were beginning to stare at them.

In the back of the boat Paddington
pulled hard on the two ropes tied
to the rudder.

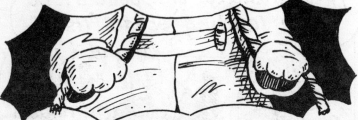

He wasn't quite sure whether Mr
Brown meant *his*, Mr Brown's, left,
or his own left, so he pulled both
just to make certain.

Everyone waited while Mr Brown
strained on the oars.

After a few minutes...

Mr Brown mopped his brow and looked crossly over his shoulder.

"I'll do it, Mr Brown," called Paddington importantly. He clambered along the side of the boat. "I'm in charge of ropes."

The Browns waited patiently while Paddington examined the rope. He wasn't very good at knots because they were rather difficult with paws. At last he announced that all was ready.

Here we go..
Cast off, Paddington.
Hold on everyone!

SPLASH

"Do what, Mr Brown?"
asked Paddington.

A picnic on the river was much
more complicated than he had
expected.

There were so many ropes to pull
he was getting a bit confused.

First of all Mr Brown told him to untie the rope. Now he had shouted to everyone to hold on.

Paddington closed his eyes and held on to the rope with both paws as tightly as he could.

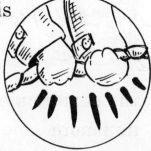

One moment he was standing on
the boat—

the next moment it wasn't there
any more.

"Henry! Paddington's fallen in the water!"

"Bear overboard!" cried Jonathan, as the boat shot away from the bank.

37

Paddington came up spluttering
for air. "I *did* hold on. That's how
I fell in."

Mrs Brown lunged into the water
with her sunshade. "Do hurry,
Henry!" she cried.

I'm sure
Paddington
can't swim

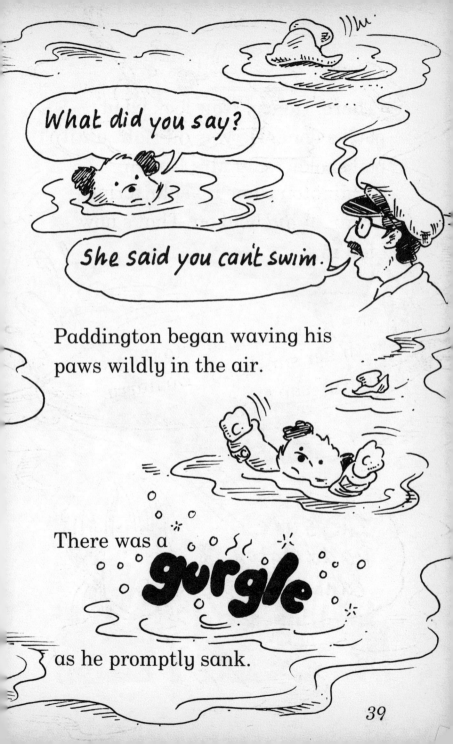

What did you say?

She said you can't swim.

Paddington began waving his paws wildly in the air.

There was a **gurgle** as he promptly sank.

"There, Henry! *Now* look what you've done. He was all right until you spoke," said Mrs Brown.

Part Four

By the time the Browns reached
the landing stage, Paddington had
already been rescued. He was
lying on his back surrounded by a
large crowd.

Everyone was staring down at him and making suggestions. The man in charge of the boats pulled his paws backwards and forwards, giving him artificial respiration.

"Thank goodness he's safe," exclaimed Mrs Brown thankfully.

"Don't see why 'e shouldn't be," said the man. "If 'e'd layed 'imself down it would only 'ave come up to 'is whiskers. The water's only about nine inches deep just 'ere. Probably a lot less now—judging by the amount 'e's swallowed."

Judy bent down and looked at Paddington. "I think he's trying to say something," she said.

Paddington sat up.

GRRRR

"Now just you lay still for a moment, young feller-me-bear," said the boatman, and pushed Paddington back down again.

"Grrr," said Paddington.

ITHINKIVELOSTMYHAT

"I THINK I'VE LOST MY HAT."

repeated the man, looking at Paddington with interest. "Is that some kind of foreign language?"

"I *come* from Peru," spluttered Paddington. "But I *live* at number thirty-two Windsor Gardens in London, and I think I've lost my hat."

"Oh, dear," said Mrs Brown. "Did you hear that, Henry? Paddington's lost his hat!"

Part Five

The Brown family stared at each
other in dismay. They often
grumbled about Paddington's
hat—but they couldn't imagine him
without it.

Paddington felt on top of his head.
"I had it on when I fell in the
water. And now it isn't there any
more."

"Gosh!" said Jonathan.
"It had so many holes
in it too! Perhaps it's sunk."

"Sunk!" cried Paddington in dismay. He ran to the edge of the landing stage and peered at the muddy water.

"He's always worn it," explained Mrs Brown to the boatman. "It was given to him by his uncle in Peru."

The boatman looked most impressed. He turned to Paddington.

You'll be wanting the Thames Conservancy, sir.

No, I don't,

said Paddington firmly.

I want my HAT.

"He means they look after the river, dear," explained Mrs Brown. "They may have found it for you."

"Once you get away from the bank the current's very strong," said the man. "It may have got swept over the weir,

if it ain't already been sucked into a whirlpool."

He pointed along the river towards a row of buildings in the distance.

Paddington gave him a hard stare. He couldn't believe his ears.

"My hat! Got sucked into a whirlpool?" he exclaimed.

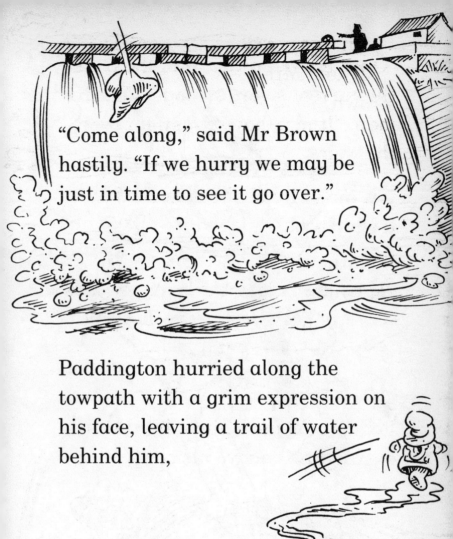

"Come along," said Mr Brown hastily. "If we hurry we may be just in time to see it go over."

Paddington hurried along the towpath with a grim expression on his face, leaving a trail of water behind him,

closely followed by...

...Mr and Mrs Brown,

Mrs Bird,

Jonathan and Judy,

the boatman

and a crowd of interested sightseers.

52

By the time they reached the weir the news had already spread. Several men in peaked caps were peering anxiously into the water.

"I hear you've lost a very valuable Persian cat," said the lock-keeper.

"Not a *cat*," said Mr Brown. "A *hat*. And it's from Peru."

"It belongs to this young bear gentleman, Fred," explained the boatman. "It's a family heirloom."

The lock-keeper scratched his head and looked at Paddington. "I've never heard of a hat being a family heirloom before. Especially a bear's heirloom."

"Mine is," said Paddington firmly. "It's a very rare sort of hat and it's got a marmalade sandwich inside. I put it in there in case of an emergency."

The lock-keeper looked more and more surprised. "Wait a minute—it wouldn't be that thing we fished out just now, would it? All sort of shapeless... like a... like a..."

"That sounds like it," said Mrs Bird.

"Herbert!" the man called to a boy nearby. "See if we've still got that wassname in the shed."

Everyone waited anxiously while Herbert disappeared into a small hut by the side of the lock. He returned after a few moments carrying a bucket.

The lock-keeper looked apologetic. "We put it in here, because we'd never seen anything like it before. We were going to send it to the museum."

VERY RARE WASSNAME

Paddington peered into the bucket. "That's not a wassname. That's my hat."

Everyone breathed a sigh of relief.

"There's a fish inside it as well," said the lock-keeper.

A fish? Inside my hat?

"That's right," said the man. "It must have been after your marmalade sandwich. Probably got in through one of the holes."

"Crikey," exclaimed Jonathan admiringly, as the Browns gathered round the bucket. "So there is!"

"That means Paddington's won the prize for catching the first fish," said Judy.

CONGRATULATIONS!

"Well, if it's some kind of competition," said the lock-keeper, "I'd better get you a jam-jar to put it in, sir.

"I suppose," he said, looking rather doubtfully at the hat, "you'll be wanting to wear it again?"

Paddington gave the lock-keeper a hard stare. He backed away and hurried off.

He returned with a jam-jar. "There you are! With the compliments of the Thames Conservancy."

"Thank you very much," said Paddington gratefully.

The man stood on the side of the lock to wave them good-bye. "It's a pleasure. After all, it's not every day we have the opportunity of saving a bear's heirloom from going over the weir. I shall remember to-day for a long time to come."

Some while later Mr Brown stopped rowing and let the boat

drift lazily downstream in the current.

It may not have been the quietest day we've ever spent on the river, but it's certainly the nicest.

The Brown family had to agree. They lay back in the boat, watched the shimmering water and listened to the music from the gramophone.

Paddington held on tightly to his
hat with one paw while he dipped
the other into a jar of his favourite
marmalade. He agreed most of all.
Now that he had got his hat back
he felt it was quite the nicest day
he'd had for a very long time.